Mr. FancyPants!

Adapted by Geof Smith • Illustrated by Caleb Meurer

Based on the screenplay "To Squarepants or Not To,"
by Luke Brookshier, Nate Cash, and Steven Banks

A GOLDEN BOOK • NEW YORK

Created by

Stephen Hillenburg

www.randomhouse.com/kids
Library of Congress Control Number: 2008908379
ISBN: 978-0-375-85121-6
Printed in the United States of America
20 19 18 17 16 15 14 13

SpongeBob opened his front door and greeted another beautiful Bikini Bottom morning.

"It's a perfect day," he said. "A perfect day for chores!"

SpongeBob loved to . . .

dust,

wash,

and vacuum.

"It's laundry day, Gary!" SpongeBob said.
He collected all his square pants—and even Gary's
pants, too—and filled the washing machine.

While the clothes were drying, Patrick called.
"Hi, SpongeBob," he said. "Listen to how long
I can whistle."

SpongeBob learned that Patrick could
whistle for a long, **long**, **long** time.

Gary got his pants out of the
dryer in time, but SpongeBob waited
too long. All his pants had shrunk!

"Gary, it looks like I need to get
new pants," SpongeBob said.
Gary said, *"Meow."*

Unfortunately, the pants store at the mall was all out of SpongeBob's style! And there wasn't going to be another shipment of square pants for *months*!

"I guess I can find a new style of pants," SpongeBob said.

"Maybe."

"Nope."

Then SpongeBob found a pair of pants he
liked. In fact, he thought they were perfect.
"They hug me like my mother!"

On the way back home, SpongeBob
ran into Patrick. "Notice anything different?"
SpongeBob asked.

"Who are you?"

"I'm SpongeBob!"

Patrick thought for a moment.

"SpongeBob has **square** pants. Now leave
me alone, you mysterious stranger."

"Patrick's so full of tartar sauce," SpongeBob said to himself. "I'm still SpongeBob! It's just a different pair of pants."

But then Sandy didn't seem to recognize him, either.

"You sure look like **Mr. FancyPants**!" she said with a laugh.

SpongeBob wasn't too worried, because
he knew that Patrick and Sandy could be
pretty silly sometimes. But when Squidward
didn't recognize him, he got scared.

(Actually, Squidward did recognize
SpongeBob. He was just trying to ignore him.)

"These pants are more powerful than I expected!" SpongeBob cried. "I guess I'm not SpongeBob SquarePants anymore. I'll have to start all over! I'm ready! I'm ready! I'M READY!"

The first thing SpongeBob FancyPants
needed was a job. So he went to the place he
knew best: the Krusty Krab.

The moment SpongeBob FancyPants walked
in, Mr. Krabs told him to get to work.

"I've got the job!" SpongeBob shouted.

"SpongeBob FancyPants has never worked here before," he said. "So you have to tell me what to do. Teach me everything you know!"

"Hmmm," Squidward whispered to himself. "Maybe I can get him fired. Then he'll leave me alone."

So SpongeBob FancyPants learned to do everything around the Krusty Krab—just the way Squidward did it.

SpongeBob ignored the customers.

And he made fun
of the food.

The Krusty Krab got messier . . .
and **messier** . . . and **MESSIER!**
And Mr. Krabs got madder . . .
and **madder** . . . and **MADDER!**

"I'm used to Squidward doing a terrible job!"
Mr. Krabs yelled. "But I expect more from *you*,
Mr. SquarePants!"

"But I can't be SpongeBob SquarePants with
ROUND PANTS on!" SpongeBob cried.

"Well, take them off," Mr. Krabs said.

"Whatever you say, Mr. Krabs!"

"I guess I'm SpongeBob **UnderPants** from now on!"